Poky's Birthday Party

Turtle Patrol Book 2

by Diana Kanan

Illustrated by Krystal and Krystel Olino

ISBN 978-1-7352616-6-9

DLK Publishing

825 N. Gould St.

Owosso, MI 48867

www.dianakanan.com

Illustrated by Krystal & Krystel Olino

Dedication

To my very "first" inspirations: Matthew, Lil Gary, Erica, Emily and Sydney. What wonderful blessings God has given.

Mom

Poky was excited for his birthday party until he realized he had to share it with dozens of brothers and sisters.

He watched as the yearlings gathered at the sandbar. Somehow his big day didn't seem special anymore.

"Where are you going?" Asked Ollie. "The party is about to start! Whale is getting ready to sing, and the dolphins are practicing their special jumps."

"What's so great about that?" Scoffed Poky. "They do that every day. Besides, I'm sure my friends at Flagler have something special planned for my birthday."

"Flagler Beach? Can I come too. . . please. . . please?" The octopus propelled himself out front. "You're in my way," Poky tried to swim around. "Besides, you'll only slow me down."

"What? I can swim faster than you." Ollie playfully wiggled his eight arms in Poky's face.

"Alright, come on." Poky giggled. After all, Ollie was his best friend.

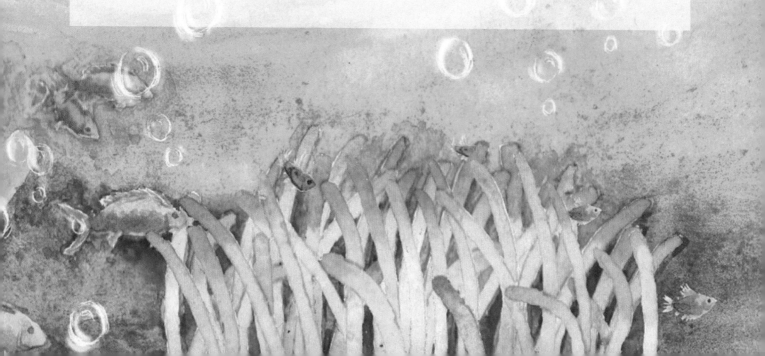

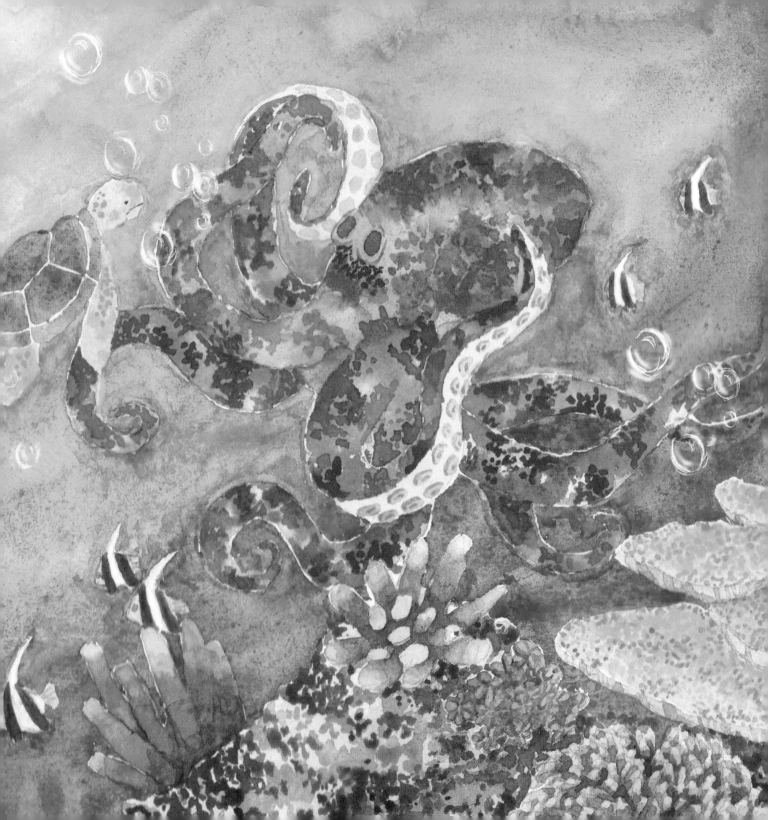

The ocean was bustling with activity as the two friends began their journey. First, Poky tried to race a fever of stingray. He lost.

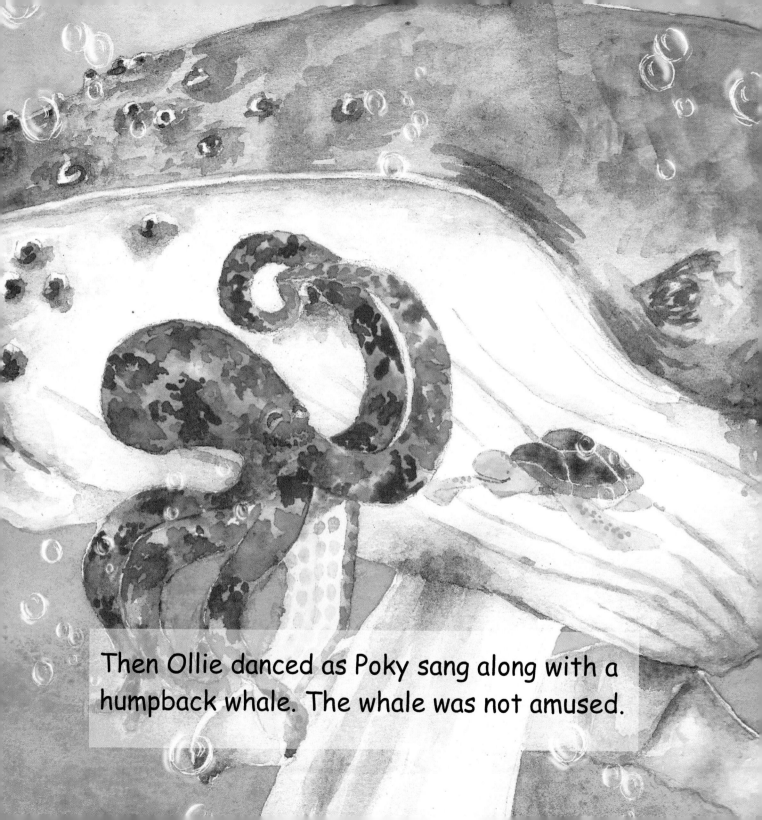

Then Ollie danced as Poky sang along with a humpback whale. The whale was not amused.

It was not all fun and games. The ocean was a wonderful playland, but it could also be a dangerous one.

"I see the beach!" poky shouted. The two began to race, but poky was having a hard time keeping up.

"Come on Poky!" Ollie shouted. "I can't," Poky was struggling to swim. "I think I am stuck!"

Ollie circled back to check on his friend and noticed plastic webbing tangled around his flippers.

He tried to free him, but the more he pulled, the more entangled Poky became. "Get help!" Poky pleaded. "Go to shore. . . ask for Stoney . . . Stoney the crab!"

Ollie began calling for help as soon as he reached the pier.

"Stoney...anyone know Stoney? Poky needs help . . . he's caught in plastic!"

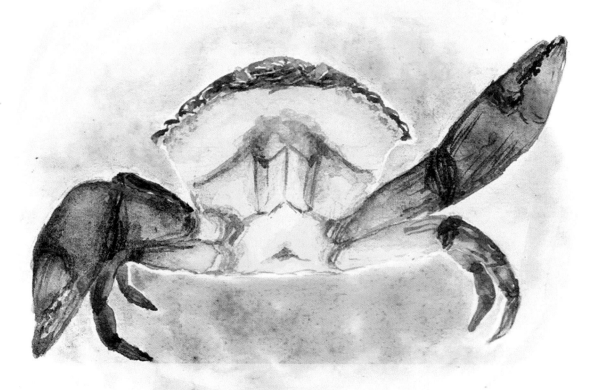

A large blue crab suddenly appeared. "Poky? Little sea turtle Poky?" The crab signaled to the seagulls perched nearby.

Stoney held on to Ollie as the seagulls led the way.
"What's Poky doing in Flagler?" Stoney asked.
"It's his birthday," Ollie said. "He wanted to
celebrate it with his Flagler friends."

The seagulls began to cirlce above when they found Poky floating upside down in a tangled mass of plastic.

Stoney used his right crushing claw to cut through the plastic around Poky's flippers while the seagulls carried the debris away. It wasn't the first time they've had to help friends hurt by plastic in the ocean.

Poky slowly opened his eyes while he carefully
stretched each flipper.
"Stoney!" He squealed in delight when he saw his old
friend. "I knew you'd come!"

"Of course I came silly. Now, let's go. I believe we have a birthday to celebrate!"

By the time they reached shore, the news of Poky's ordeal had spread throughout Flagler. His old friends, clam, snail, starfish, and jellyfish had built the biggest sandcastle cake Poky and Ollie had ever seen.

The birthday celebration lasted late into the evening as they played games and shared silly stories. Ollie even made some new Flagler friends down by the dock.

Just as the party was winding down they heard a commotion nearby.

"Look!" Stoney shouted. "A turtle hatch!"
They turned to a batch of baby turtles
poking their heads through the sand.

Everyone cheered while Poky helped patrol the baby sea turtles into their new home.

"Happy birthday! Happy birthday! Happy birthday!" Poky shouted.

Ollie joined Poky to watch the last baby sea turtle disappear into the night.

"I'm sorry Poky," he said sadly. "I know you wanted this to be your special day and now you have to share it with even more sea turtles."

Poky smiled and looked back at his friends.

"I was wrong Ollie. It wasn't my birthday that made this day special. What made it special is that I got to share it with anyone at all."

A Word From the Author

I truly hope you enjoyed *Poky's Birthday Party* as much as I enjoyed writing it. My goal is to create entertaining children's stories that bring awareness of plastic pollution and the effects it has on our oceans and marine life.

When we know better, we do better. ~ Maya Angelou

FREE Sea Turtle Coloring Pages

www.dianakanan.com

Statistics

Over 1 million marine animals (including mammals, fish, sharks, turtles, and birds) are killed each year due to plastic debris in the ocean according to the Sea Turtle Conservancy in Gainesville, Florida. They also state that currently, it is estimated that there are 100 million tons of plastic in oceans around the world.

How You Can Help

Education is important to solving marine pollution. The public can get involved in this issue by:

- Reduce, Reuse and Recycle plastics;
- Use reusable cloth bags instead of plastic bags when shopping;
- Support local, regional and nationwide bans on plastic grocery bags;
- Don't litter. Instead, volunteer at local beach clean-up events;
- Make sure to properly secure your garbage to prevent any fly-away plastics;
- Don't release balloons into the air. They travel far and end up in our oceans being consumed by sea turtles that mistake them for food.

Author's Bookshelf

As an Amazon best-selling author of *Poky the Turtle Patrol*, Diana is dedicated to bringing awareness of the endangered sea turtle. The author donates a portion of all book proceeds to the Volusia/Flagler Turtle Patrol.

Poky the Turtle Patrol

Available on Amazon

Visit the author at www.dianakanan.com

Sign up to become a member of Poky's Turtle Patrol to receive special offers and give-a-ways.

Made in the USA
Middletown, DE
31 May 2022

66439680R00024